Dear Cameron
Wishing you a very
happy first birthday
With love from
Auntie Marianne
Uncle Tom
Elodie &
Joshua

17
June
2018
x

This book belongs to:

....

AN ANIMAL ABC

Originally screen printed by hand by
The Print Block,
Whitstable

First published in the United Kingdom in 2016 by
Pavilion Children's Books
1 Gower Street
London, WC1E 6HD

An imprint of Pavilion Books Company Limited.

ISBN: 9781843653134

A CIP catalogue record for this book is available from the British Library.

10 9 8 7 6 5 4 3 2 1

Reproduction by Mission Productions, Hong Kong
Printed by 1010 Printing International Ltd., China

This book can be ordered directly from the publisher online at www.pavilionbooks.com, or try your local bookshop.

AN ANIMAL ABC

by Alice Pattullo

PAVILION

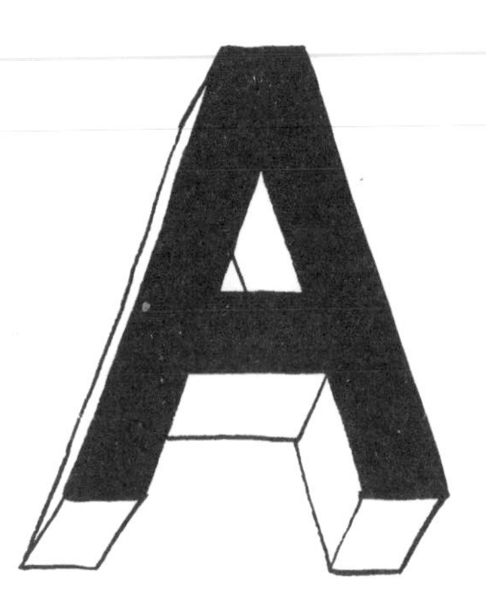

is for armadillo,
short, stout and round.

The armadillo is one of the few mammals in the world with a shell of hard, bony plates all over its body. Its name in Spanish means 'little armoured one'.

ARMADILLO

CINGULATA

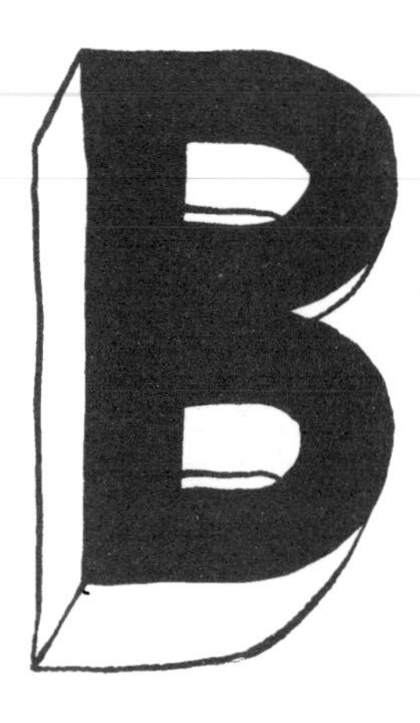

is for beetle,
close to the ground.

One out of every four animals on Earth is a beetle. Beetles have a hard exoskeleton, meaning their bones are on the outside. The insect can be found in nearly every habitat on the globe, apart from the freezing polar extremes.

BEETLE

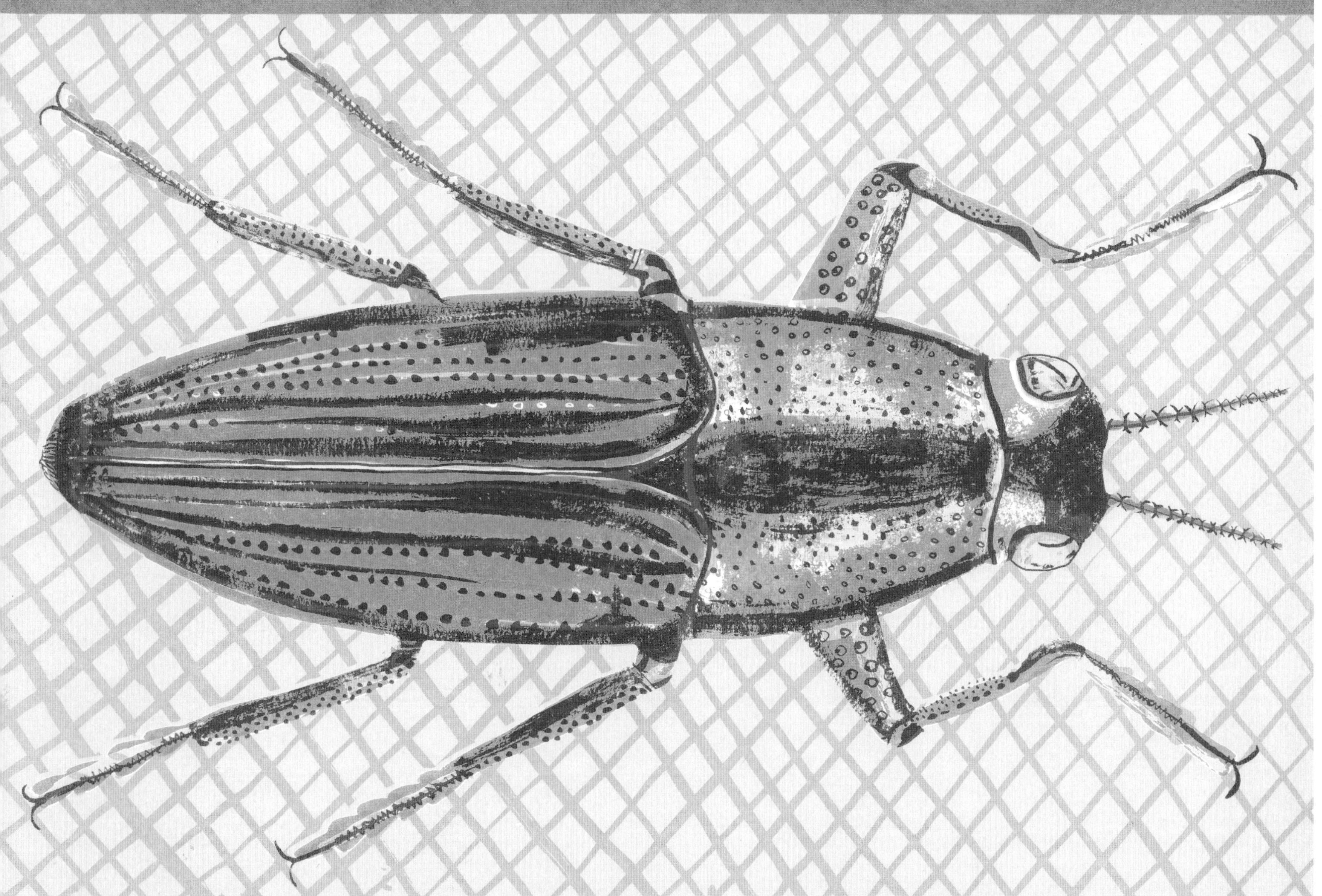

COLEOPTERA

is for crab,
crawling on the seabed.

Crabs communicate with each other by drumming their pincer claws or waving them in the air. A group of crabs is called a 'cast'.

BRACHYURA

is for dove,
flying home overhead.

The white dove carries great significance in many cultures and religions. These birds are released into the air as a symbol of love, peace and hope.

DOVE
STREPTOPELIA DECAOCTO

is for elephant,
trunk, tail and tusk.

The largest land animal in the world has a mighty mind, too. The creature's enormous brain size means that it has great intelligence and an amazing memory. Elephants can use their trunks like an arm and their big ears can be used like a fan to cool themselves down.

ELEPHANT

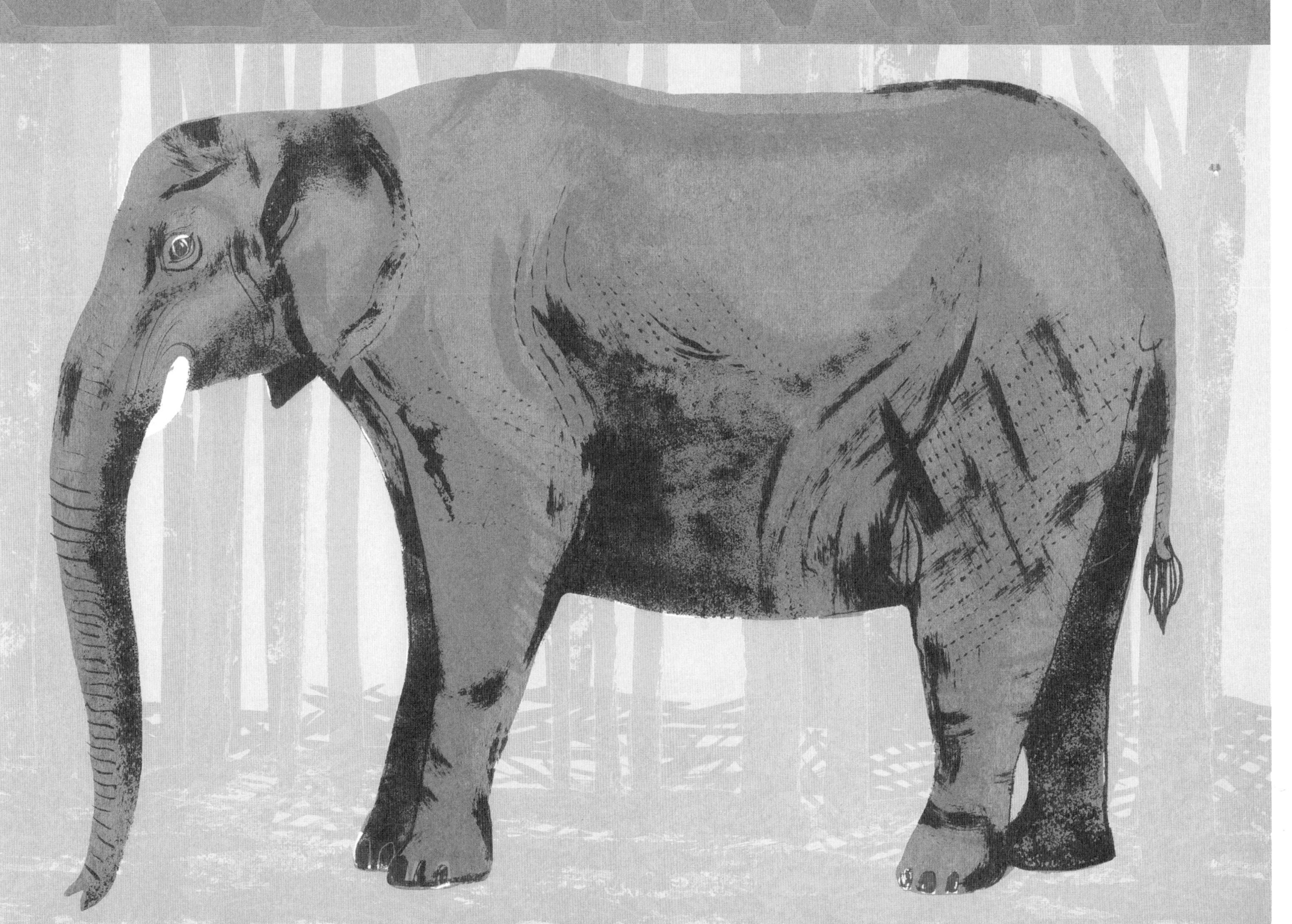

elephantidae

is for fox,
roaming in the dusk.

The fox is the most widespread species of wild dog on the planet.
Unlike other dogs, however, the fox is able to retract its claws just like a cat does.

FOX

CANIDAE

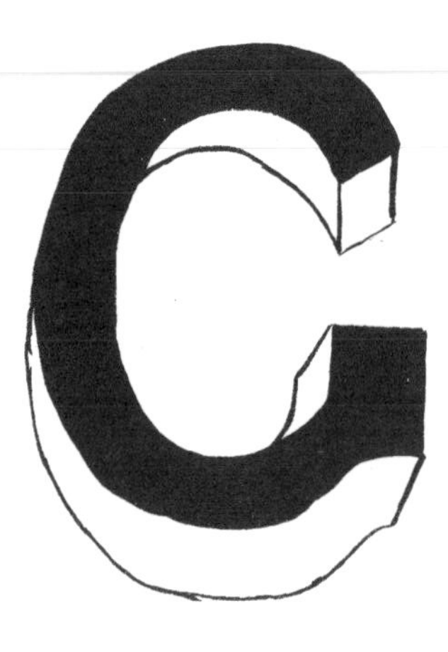

is for grizzly,
a most fearsome bear.

Grizzly bears are awe-inspiring, solitary giants. They are known to be expert hunters, and their bite is so strong it could crush a bowling ball, but much of their diet is made up of nuts, roots and berries.

GRIZZLY BEAR

ursus arctos

is for hippo,
in his watery lair.

The ancient Greeks named the hippopotamus 'river horse'. It has evolved to have small legs as they are lighter in water. The mammal can spend up to sixteen hours a day submerged in the water.

HIPPOPOTAMUS

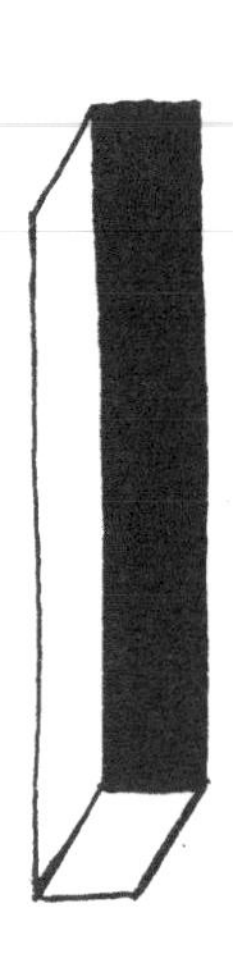

is for iguana,
curled in the sun.

There are many species of iguana, with almost as many types of behaviour.
Some scramble across desert and plains, while others live high up in rainforest trees.

IGUANA

IGUANA

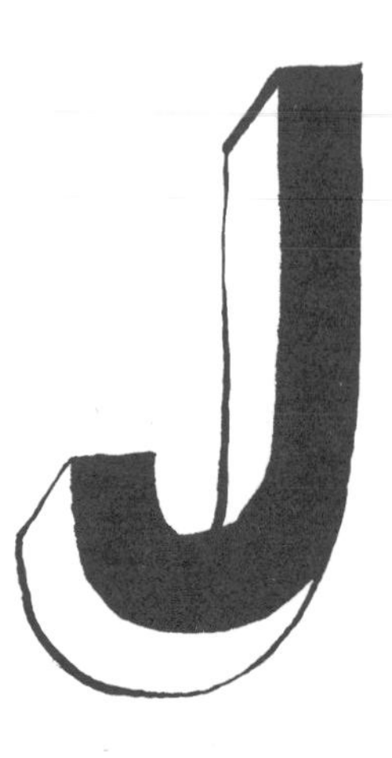

is for jackrabbit,
ready to run.

Despite its name, the jackrabbit is actually a hare, not a rabbit. It has huge, tapered ears and a powerful pair of back legs.

JACK RABBIT

lepus californicus

is for kangaroo,
taking hop, skip and bound.

Kangaroos have very strong legs for leaping and use their long tails for balance. On land, kangaroos move their hind legs together as they jump. In the water, they are able to paddle each leg independently.

KANGAROO

macropus rufus

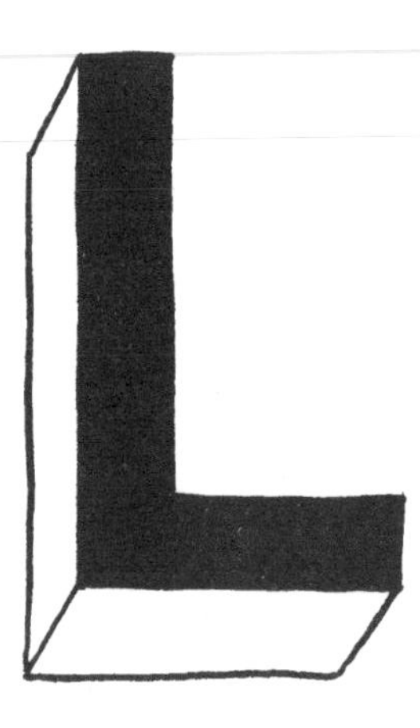

is for leopard,
sprinting the ground.

The leopard can run very fast – up to 58kph. The big cat is just as graceful leaping between tree branches as it is on the ground. Its eye-catching spots are known as 'rosettes'.

LEOPARD

panthera pardus

is for moth,
who flits to the light.

The moth is active at night – that is why its wings are usually softer and duller than a butterfly's. They are masters of disguise.

MOTH

lepidoptera

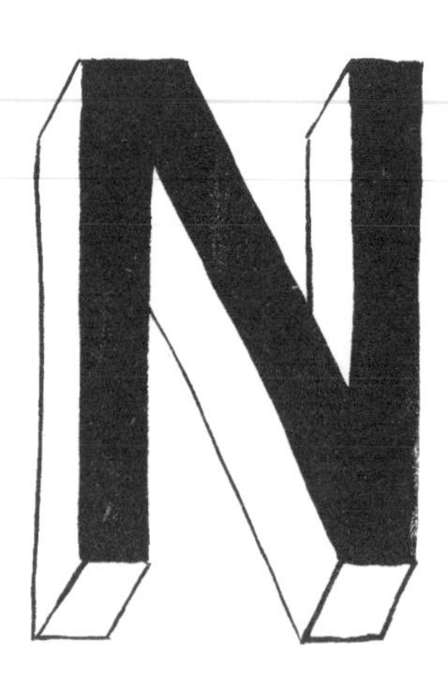

is for nautilus,
hidden out of sight.

The nautilus is an ancient and mysterious creature. The animal has lived undisturbed in the oceans for millions of years and is considered a living fossil. Its shell is divided into chambers and it can have up to 90 tentacles.

NAUTILUS

nautilidae

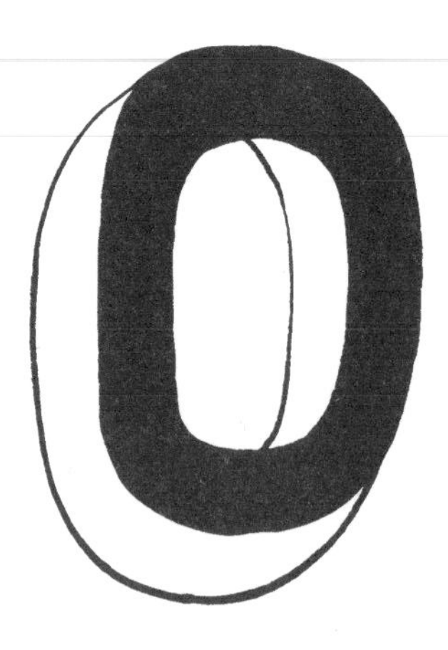

is for okapi,
with stripes tail to toe.

The curious okapi is the only living relative of the giraffe, although it has stripes similar to a zebra. The mammal has scent glands on its foot, allowing it to mark its territory as it roams.

okapia johnstoni

is for polar bear,
striding through snow.

The polar bear has two layers of fur to help it keep warm in the cold of the North Pole. In summer, if the air gets above freezing, polar bears can overheat. The giants will roll in the snow or take a swim to cool off. Their Latin name means 'sea bear'.

POLAR BEAR

ursus maritimus

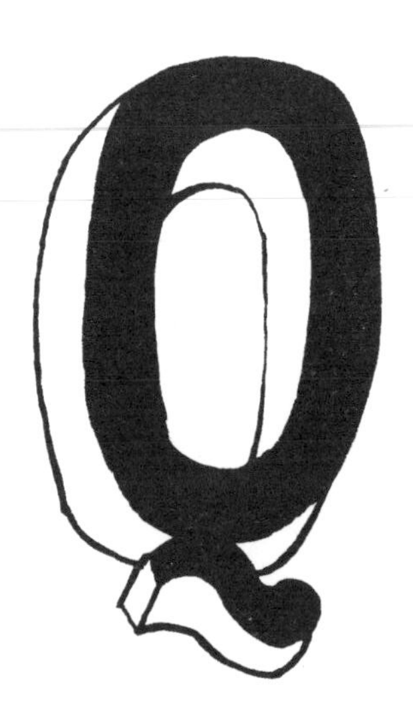

is for quail,
with flamboyant head feather.

The quail lays its eggs in nests on the ground. Once hatched, the chicks will walk in a line, following the mother bird. Quails can fly only a short distance.

QUAIL

ondontophoridae

is for rhino,
with skin of tough leather.

Although rhino skin is weathered and thick, it is sensitive to sunburn and insect bites. The creatures wallow in mud to keep themselves protected.

RHINOCEROS

rhinocerotidae

is for sloth,
who smiles while asleep.

The sloth is a tree dweller. It moves so slowly that algae and fungi are able to grow on its fur. This helps the mammal stay camouflaged amongst the branches. Sloths also have long curved claws to help them hang from trees with little effort.

SLOTH

bradypodidae

is for turtle,
who swims waters deep.

Although the turtle lives at sea, it lays its eggs on land. Sea turtles have flat, streamlined shells to help them glide through the water.

TURTLE

chelonioidea

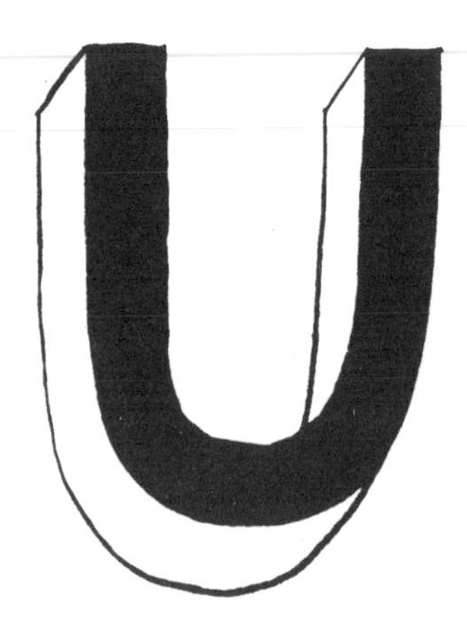

is for uakari,
through branches it glides.

The uakari has a bright crimson face, a bald head and a cry that sounds like laughter. Unlike most monkeys, it only has a short tail, so uses its arms and legs to climb instead.

UAKARI

is for viper,
who slithers and slides.

There are over 200 species of viper. The snake's hollow fangs are filled with deadly venom. Surprisingly, vipers are not found in Australia.

VIPER

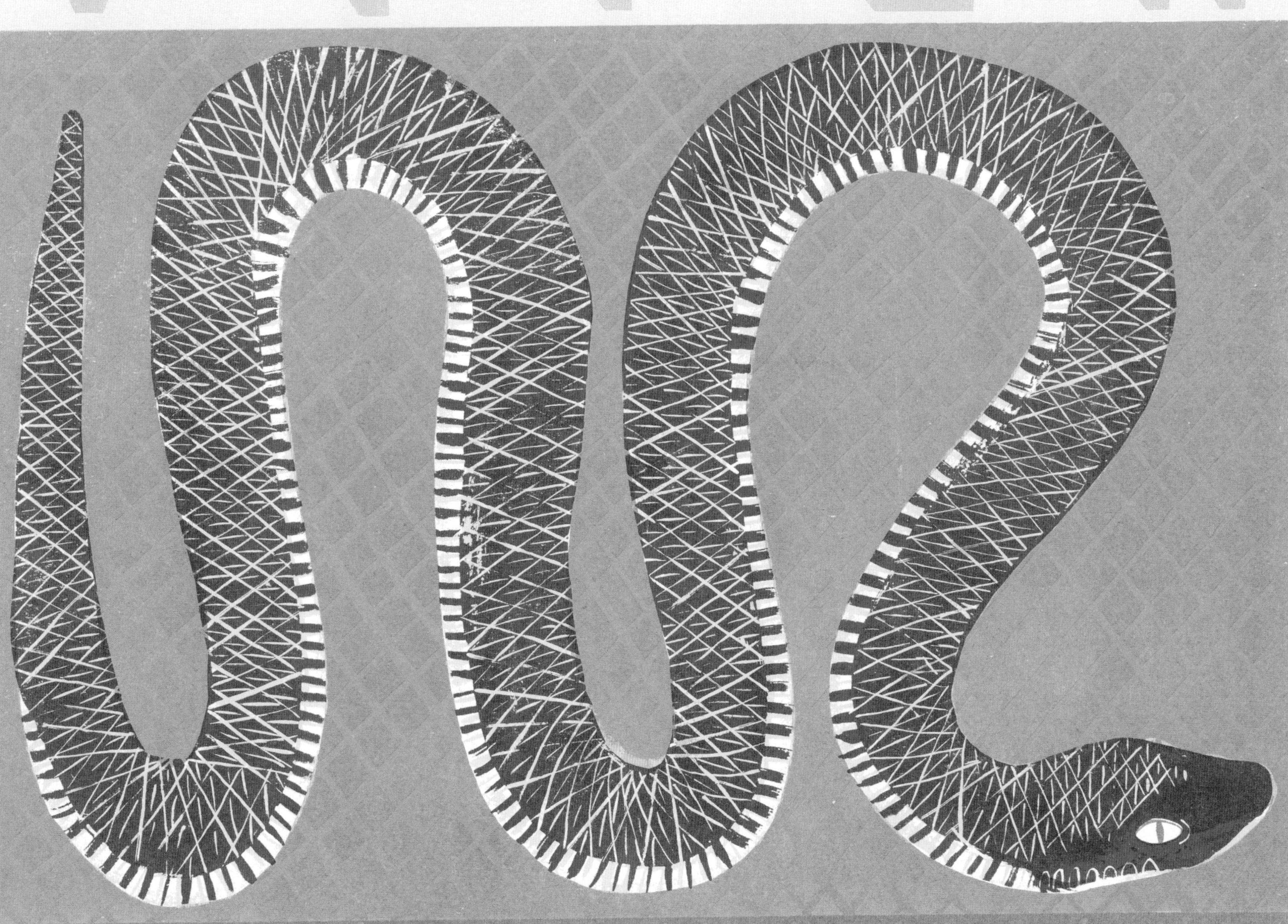

VIPERIDAE

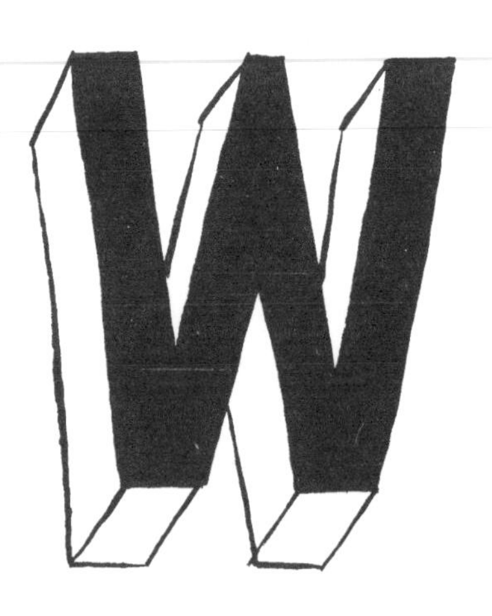

is for whale,
the biggest of all.

The blue whale is an undersea colossus. Its tongue alone can weigh as much as an elephant.
The whale feeds on tiny marine life called 'krill'.

WHALE

CETACEA

is for Xantus,
so quiet and small.

Xantus's hummingbird uses its curved beak to feed on nectar from flowers.
The hum of this bird comes from the way it flaps its wings very fast, almost fifty times per second.

XANTUS

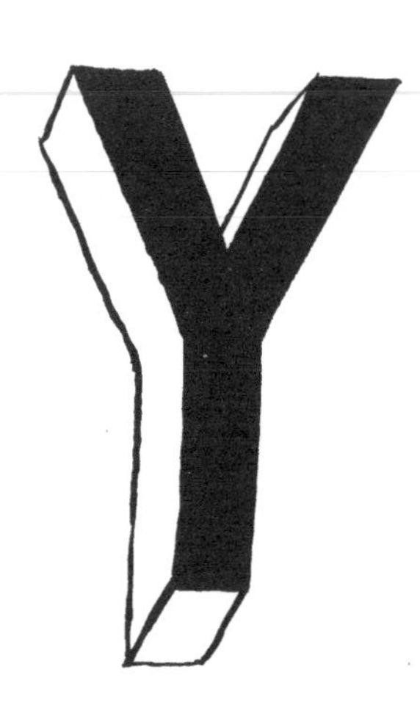

is for yak,
long mane and great might.

The yak wanders the steppes of the Himalayas, living at the highest altitude of any mammal.
Its split, cloven hoof helps it climb safely over icy ground.

YAK

bos grunniens

is for zebra,
striped black and white.

Zebras stick together in herds. The black and white stripes are unique to each individual animal, like a fingerprint is to humans. The bold stripes on their coat make it difficult for a predator to pick out a single animal to chase.

equus quagga

That brings us to
the end of this animal ABC,
and completes the marvellous,
mixed-up menagerie.

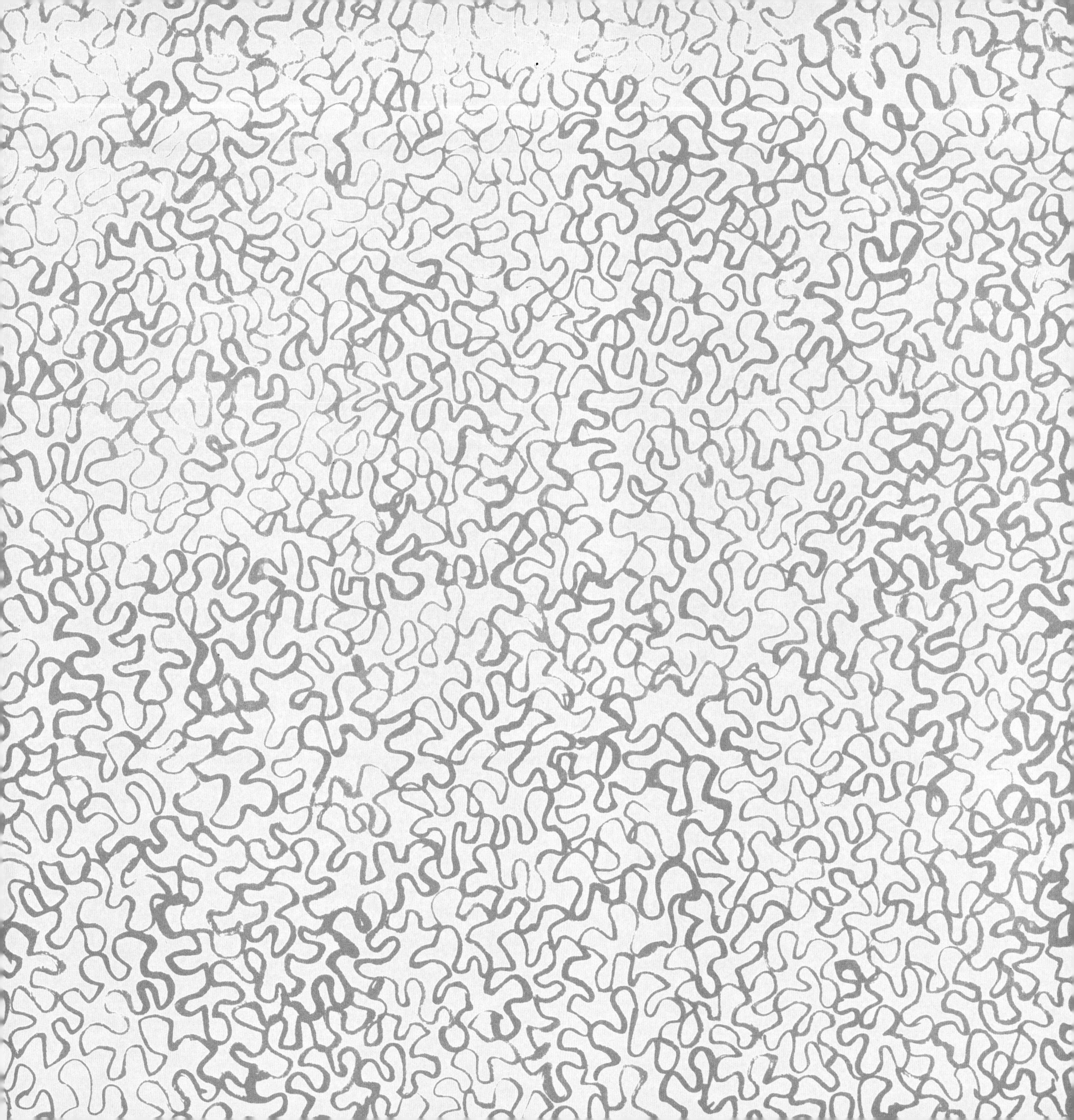

Creature Features

Shown on these pages are details from all of the animals contained in this book.
Can you find which detail belongs to which animal?
We've provided the first answer for you.

1. JackRabbit

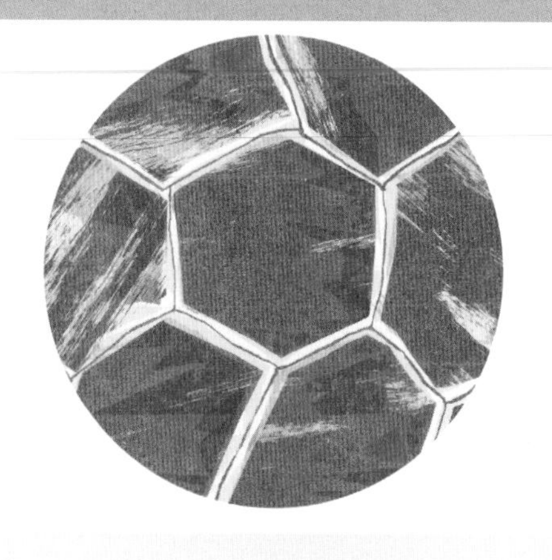

2. ________________

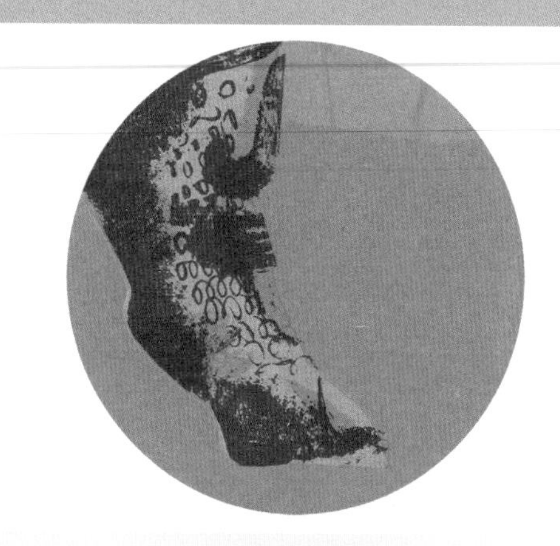

3. ________________

4. ________________

5. ________________

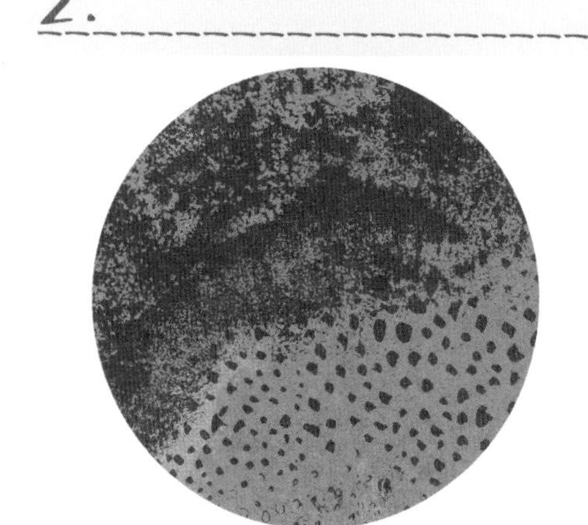

6. ________________

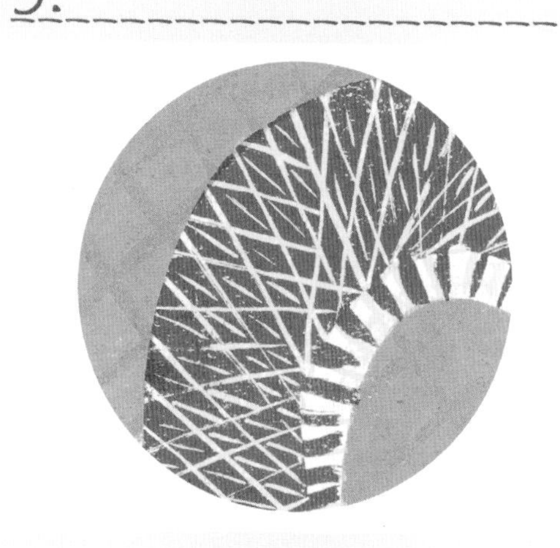

7. ________________

8. ________________

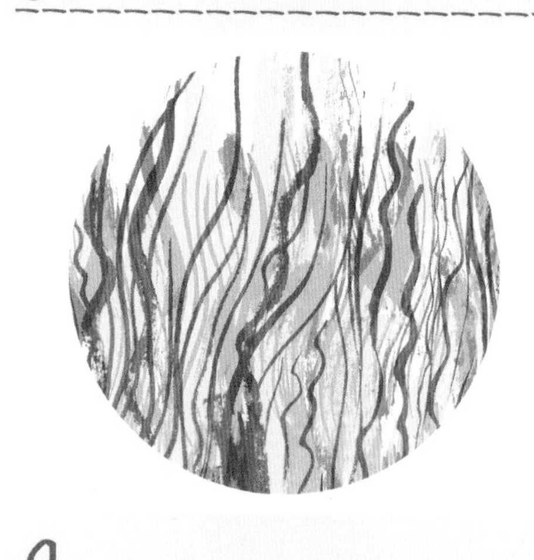

9. ________________

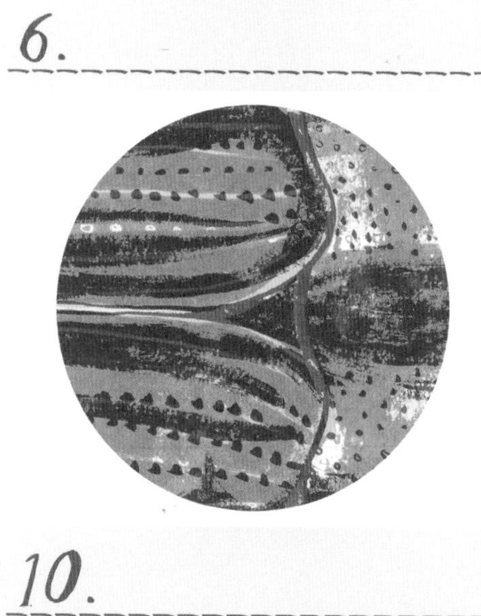

10. ________________

11. ________________

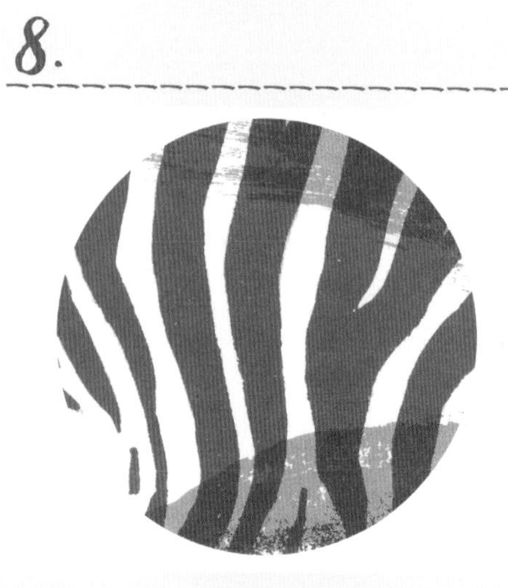

12. ________________

13. ________________

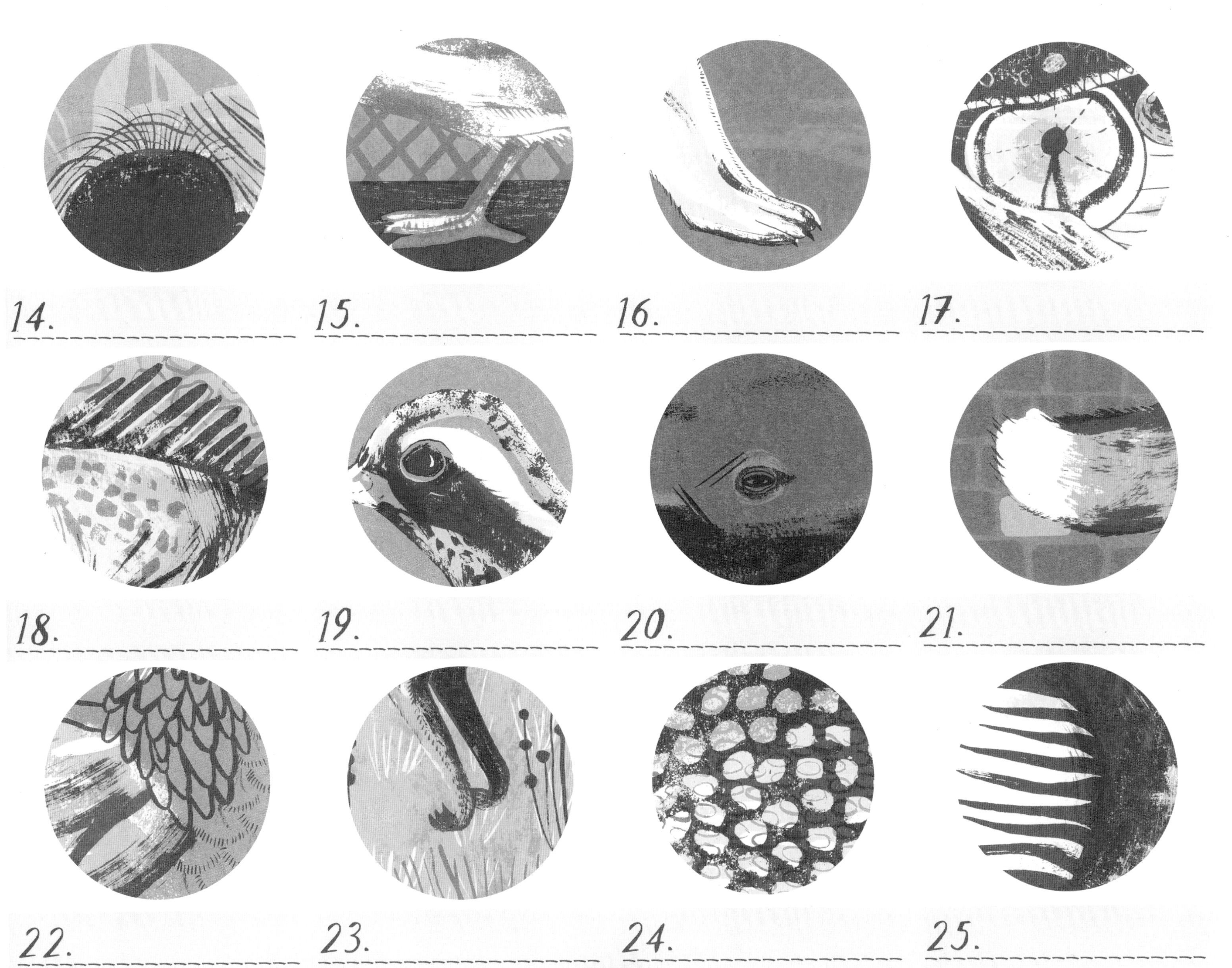

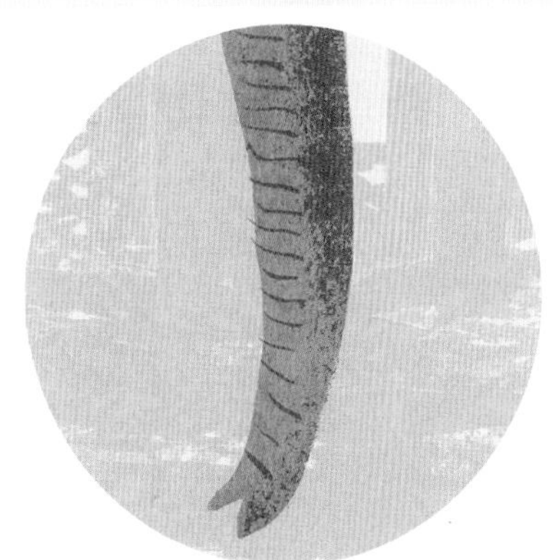

26.

Turn the page to see the answers!

About the author

Alice Pattullo is an illustrator based in East London. Alice originally hails from the North East where she was brought up in a creative household and encouraged to draw and be messy from a very young age… which she now relishes being able to do as part of her job.

When she was younger Alice's family always had a pet cat in tow, which is one of the reasons why Alice likes animals so much. Over the years there was Lucifer (the devil's cat), Max (the mad one), Min and Fido (fat and thin), Lily and Fred (soft and sharp), Syd (the crazy kitten) and last but not in the slightest bit least, Betty, who still leaves her white fur on the patchwork quilt on the windowsill in Newcastle and has a favourite bit of green string to play with.

Alice mainly produces illustrations for commissioned briefs for a variety of outcomes including editorial, packaging and museum display. Alongside this Alice produces limited edition screen prints which she sells and exhibits at various shops and galleries across the UK. She enjoys producing work exploring themes of British tradition, folklore and superstition. Research is often at the heart of her practice and she is increasingly interested in using text and rhyme in her work, often using snippets of old folk songs, playground verse, or obscure proverbs to make up part of her prints.

This project was a slight departure for Alice – intending to be a side project to just experiment with drawing and different mark-making techniques without being tied down by deadlines or working to a commissioned brief, but it soon became a two year labour of love, with each animal coming to represent a letter in the alphabet along with its scientific name. Alice enjoyed learning unusual facts about each animal along the way – like the fact that an armadillo can jump almost six feet high and a polar bear can smell a seal from up to a mile away!

As an illustrator, Alice works predominantly with brush and indian ink to paint fine lines and details in her drawings, sometimes using white ink to work negatively into black silhouettes. Combined with this, Alice paints up marks, patterns and textures to cut out and collage back into her work – she finds it particularly fun to try and make the perfect texture for the armadillo's back or just the right pattern for the viper's scaly skin for example. From her black and white drawings, Alice then splits her image into separate layers so each layer can be printed in a different colour to form a bright and colourful screenprint. For this project each animal was made up of four layers equalling four colours. Each layer was painstakingly printed by hand by Suki at The Print Block in Whitstable to produce the finished limited edition prints that make up the basis of this book.

Acknowledgements

I'd like to thank Suki Hayes Watkins at The Print Block for all the hard graft of screen printing the full original alphabet series (over 3000 pulls involved…) and Mandy Archer for helping with editing the text for this book.

A big thank you to friends and family who put up with me listing animals and rhymes while putting the ABC together – you know who you are.

Answers to Creature Features quiz

(pages 60-61)

1 jackrabbit; 2 turtle; 3 rhinoceros; 4 sloth; 5 moth; 6 hippopotamus; 7 viper; 8 grizzly bear; 9 yak; 10 beetle; 11 leopard; 12 zebra; 13 crab; 14 uakari; 15 dove; 16 polar bear; 17 nautilus; 18 iguana; 19 Xantus's hummingbird; 20 whale; 21 fox; 22 quail; 23 kangaroo; 24 armadillo; 25 okapi; 26 elephant.